Four Arrows & Magpie

A KIOWA STORY

HAWK
PUBLISHING
GROUP
TULSA

Four Arrows & Magpie

A KIOWA STORY

N. Scott Momaday

Library of Congress Cataloging-in-Publication Data

Momaday, N. Scott
Four Arrows and Magpie: A Kiowa Story / N. Scott Momaday

ISBN 1-930709-63-3

Library of Congress Control Number: 2006930852

Published in the United States by
HAWK Publishing Group.

HAWK Publishing Group
7107 South Yale Avenue #345
Tulsa, OK 74136
918-492-3677
hawkpub.com

HAWK and colophon are trademarks
belonging to the HAWK Publishing Group.

Interior and Cover Design by
Müllerhaus Publishing Arts, Inc.
MullerhausPubArts.com

Printed in the United States of America.
9 8 7 6 5 4 3 2 1

For Baylee
and all the daughters of Oklahoma

Akeah-de. They were camping.

A long time ago, there lived a people on the Great Plains of the North American continent. They lived in a land that is now called Oklahoma. The people and the land are still there, but, a long time ago, their world was a very different place. There were no roads or fences, no automobiles or telephones, no towns or farmhouses. The land was vast and beautiful, full of wildflowers and waving grasses, high floating clouds and brilliant rainbows. Then, as now, the sun was at home on the plains, and at sunrise and sunset the land and the sky came together in magic splendor.

The people lived a free and happy life. They lived in tepees, cone-shaped structures made of animal skins that were stretched over a framework of long poles. In the daylight, the tepees were like sails on the sea of grasses. At night, when fires were lighted in the tepees so the people inside could cook their food and be warm, the tepees glowed like lanterns in the darkness.

The tepees were set close together and made a camp, a Kiowa camp. The Kiowa people had come from the north many years before, from the mountains above the Yellowstone River in a land now called Montana. Some of the old people in the camp could remember hearing the story of the journey from their grandparents. The people of the camp loved the story, for it was their story, the story of who they were.

The story the grandparents told always began in the same way:

"*Akeah-de*. They were camping. Long, long ago and far, far away, our ancestors lived in a dark world, a dense forest in which they could hardly see through the trees. But even then, even there, they moved about, feeling their way from place to place, trying to see through the darkness. Then one day they came to a river. A hollow log lay on the bank. There was a strange, faint glow coming from the nearest end. They looked into the log, and, at the other end was a brilliant light. One by one they entered the log and crawled through it, and one by one they emerged into this present world, the world in which we now live, this bright and beautiful world that is abundant with the good things of life. They called themselves *kwuda*, 'coming out.' That is who we are, the coming-out people. In time, our name became *Kiowa*.

In the camp lived a boy, whose name was Four Arrows, and his twin

sister, whose name was Magpie. Four Arrows and Magpie loved the life

they lived in the camp. There were other children to play with, brave and

beautiful men and women to admire, and old people to listen to, for the

old people were very wise, and they told the best stories. And also in the

camp were many horses and dogs. Four Arrows and Magpie loved the

newborn puppies and foals especially. They were soft and furry or velvety

to the touch, and, like Four Arrows and Magpie, they loved to play.

10

Outside the camp, in the great open plain, were wild creatures—rabbits and prairie dogs, turtles and coyotes, every sort of bird, large and small, and of course the great herds of buffalo. The Kiowas loved the buffalo and the horse above all other animals, for the buffalo gave them meat to eat and hides to make shelter and clothing, and the horse gave them freedom to roam and strength to transport their belongings. The world in which Four Arrows and Magpie lived was whole, alive, and beautiful.

There were brave warriors in the camp, men who were

excellent horsemen, hunters and soldiers. The bravest

of the warriors was Charging Bear. He was tall, and

handsome, with raven black hair and skin the

color of bronze. He carried a powerful shield.

Every boy in the camp wanted to be a warrior

like Charging Bear, especially Four Arrows.

And every girl dreamed of having a

brother like him, especially Magpie.

13

Four Arrows and Magpie loved to see Charging Bear walk through the camp. He was tall and straight, and his stride was long and steady. Although he appeared to look straight ahead, the children knew that his eyesight was as sharp as an eagle's, and that he saw everything around him. He belonged to the society of warriors called the "Real Dogs." The society was composed of only ten men, the bravest warriors, and Charging Bear was their leader.

Everywhere he walked, there followed at his heels his beloved dog, Hunter. Although the time had passed when dogs could talk, Hunter could express himself very well.

Sometimes, when Charging Bear sat in council with the chiefs,

Four Arrows and Magpie would dare to approach his tepee. They

approached with wonder and deep respect, for outside the tepee,

hanging on a tripod, was Charging Bear's

shield. It was a famous shield, decorated with

eagle feathers and the image of a great bear,

encircled with bear tracks. The twins did not

come too close to it, for its power was alive and

mysterious. Four Arrows came a step closer than

his sister, for he dreamed of being a great warrior,

and of having such a shield himself. Magpie gazed

upon the shield with wonder and admiration. She was full of pride for

her brother and for Charging Bear and his great shield. And she was

proud of Hunter too, and believed him to be, like his master, a member

of the warrior society. After all, he was beyond question a "real dog."

17

That summer all was peaceful at the camp. There was happy talk and laughter, singing and dancing. The earth was beautiful under the sun and moon, the air was fresh with gentle rains, and the grass and wildflowers made a brilliant carpet on the rolling land. But suddenly, one day, everything changed. The peace and happiness of the camp were shattered. A man came running in from the plain, shouting "Fire! Fire!" Everyone began to run and cry out. There was a terrible commotion. In the distance there rose up a long line of black smoke, and then on the horizon flames appeared. It was a prairie fire, raging and racing toward the camp. People were running in every direction, looking for their children, gathering their belongings, or trying to catch the frightened, stampeding horses. The dogs were barking and howling, and turning in circles. The line of flames and smoke came nearer and nearer, and there was the smell of scorched grass and the sound of fire crackling.

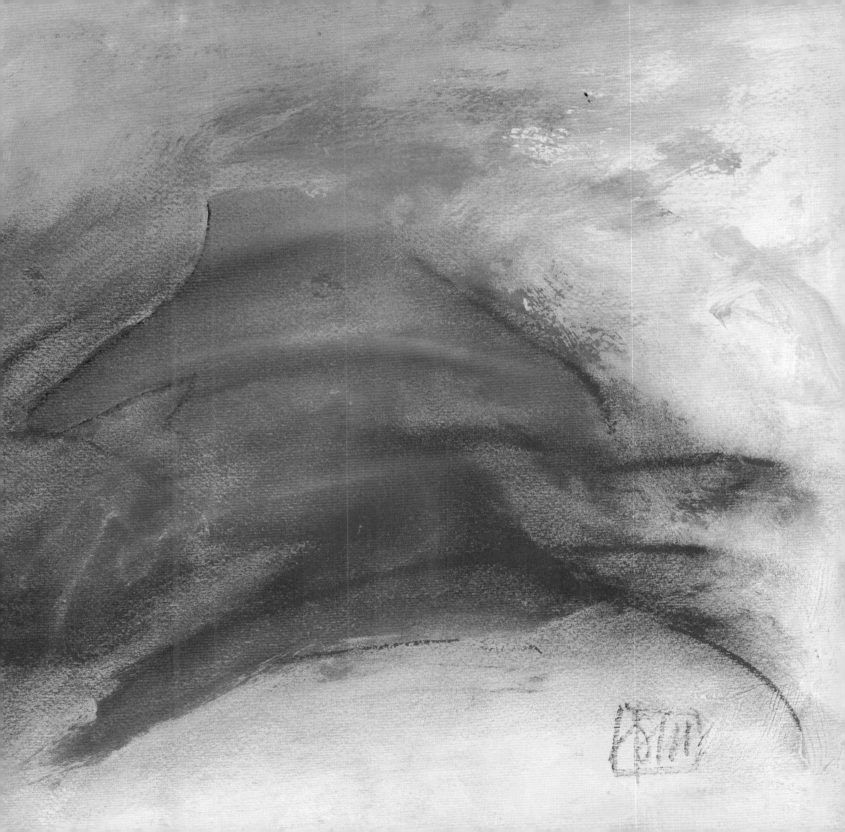

Watching the terrible scene, Four Arrows and Magpie were truly

frightened, and huddled together, unable to move. And then a shadow

fell over them and a voice sounded just above them. It was

the voice of Charging Bear. It was calm, full of assurance,

as full of power as his shield. "The other warriors and

I are going to fight the fire. You two must go that way,

quickly." He pointed toward the river.

"Where is Hunter?" Magpie asked.

"I don't know," Charging Bear answered. "But you must go, now!

You must go to safety, to the river!" And he was gone,

running with his long strides straight into

the fire and smoke.

Four Arrows and Magpie began to run, hand in hand. But after a few steps, Four Arrows stopped. "You go ahead," he said to Magpie. "There is something I must do. I will catch up with you." He raced back among the tepees.

Magpie ran ahead, dreadfully concerned for her

brother. Once she turned to look back. The fire was

now more visible above the camp. It seemed a giant,

writhing, snake-like beast, twisting, undulating,

roaring. And there, at its nearest point, crouching

and facing it in the grass, was Hunter! Magpie could not

believe her eyes! Hunter was standing fast, like a warrior,

in the face of the fire.

Magpie ran back until she was
sure that Hunter could hear
her voice above the sound
of the fire, and she called to
him, "Come, Hunter, come!
This way! Now!" Hunter
turned, looked at her with
an expression of great
gladness, and ran to her,
wagging his tail wildly.
And at the same moment Four Arrows joined
them. He was carrying Charging Bear's shield.

The warriors had fought the fire, and diverted it from the

camp, but a great tongue of flame raced down toward the river.

It licked at the twins and at Hunter, and they ran as fast as they

could until they were out of breath, and then they ran again.

They fell exhausted on the bank of the river, just as the flames came for them. And they rolled into the cool, running water of the river and were safe. It was like a dream.

When the nightmare of fire had passed, and they caught their breath, the twins saw that they were standing in the river shallows, beside a hollow log that lay on the bank, one end near the water. Magpie was holding Hunter, and Four Arrows was holding the great shield. Above them on the bank stood the tall, straight figure of Charging Bear. He was smiling down at them with eyes that spoke, without words, of love and gratitude.

One by one Magpie, Four Arrows, and Hunter climbed up through the hollow log and came into the world above, and Charging Bear, with Hunter at his heels, led the children back to the camp.

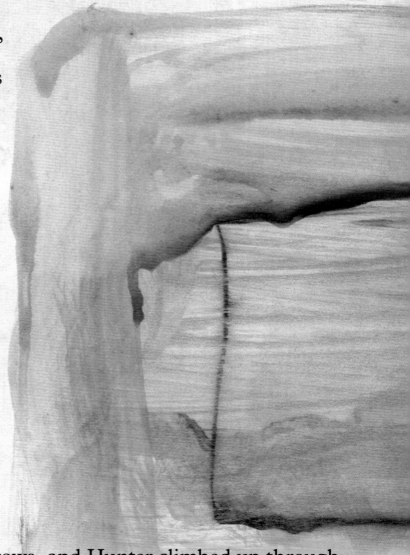

29

Later, at the end of that long, long day, Charging Bear made an honor song for the twins, and he sang, *"You saved my beloved dog, Hunter, and you saved my shield. You are as brave as the bravest warriors, and you have earned shields of your own.*

I will make you, Four Arrows, a shield with my own hands, and

I will make you, Magpie, a shield with my own hands. These will be

the shields of the coming-out children, and they will be honored by us all,

by all the coming-out people."

And so it was. *Akeah-de.*

ABOUT THE AUTHOR

The Pulitzer Prize is the highest honor in the literary world. In 1969 the Pulitzer Prize for Fiction went to *House Made of Dawn,* a first novel written by a Kiowa Indian born in Lawton, Oklahoma who spent the first year of his life at his grandparents' home on Kiowa land, where his father was born and raised. N. Scott Momaday would grow up largely on reservations in the Southwest, far from mainstream centers of education.

Although a relatively unknown author at the time he won the Pulitzer, America and the world soon realized the depth of N. Scott Momaday's talent. A renowned novelist, poet, painter, and scholar, his artistic works have encompassed a panorama as wide as the landscapes he commemorates.

Momaday's poems, plays, novels, folk tales, memoirs, and children's books have earned him the respect of the international community while illuminating the Native traditions that inspire his work. His words and life have helped reconnect contemporary readers with the understanding his forefathers had of the cherished bond between humankind and nature.

Momaday is the founder and chairman of The Buffalo Trust, a nonprofit foundation dedicated to supporting indigenous communities' efforts to preserve and perpetuate their cultural identity. He is also the founder of the nonprofit Rainy Mountain Foundation in Oklahoma, which is building an archive and camp for Native American youth at Rainy Mountain, Oklahoma.

The purpose of the Oklahoma Arts Institute (OAI) is to provide programs of excellence in arts education for Oklahoma and the region in order to develop future artists and art audiences while enhancing the quality of life for all Oklahomans.

Since 1976, the OAI has recruited nationally-renowned artists to teach fine arts programs for talented Oklahoma youth and continuing education workshops for adults. Oklahoma high school students are selected through a statewide competitive audition process for a two-week, intensive summer arts academy. Each fall, educators, professional artists, and students gather for four-day weekend workshops in the literary, visual, and performing arts. In 1991, the Oklahoma legislature passed a joint resolution designating the Institute "Oklahoma's Official School of the Arts."

The Oklahoma Arts Institute is part of a unique public/private partnership. Major funding is provided by private donors secured by the Oklahoma Arts Institute, with matching funds from the Oklahoma State Department of Education and additional support from the Oklahoma Arts Council and the Oklahoma Department of Tourism and Recreation. The generosity of Institute donors provides scholarships for the high school students and teachers.

In 1906, ONEOK's founders began providing safe, reliable energy to Oklahomans. Today, they continue the tradition of excellence and community involvement, celebrating 100 years of service to our great state.

This book is one of three published as a joint endeavor of ONEOK, the Oklahoma Centennial Commission, and the Institute in order to commemorate Oklahoma's one hundredth birthday and proudly lead the way into the next century.

These worthwhile projects are the cornerstones of a renewed commitment to support Oklahoma literature and authors. All profits generated from the books will be used to publish additional projects that bring to life the heart and soul of Oklahoma.